Pixie Magic

Dotty and the
Sweet Surprise

Special thanks to Valerie Wilding
For Matthew McIntosh

ORCHARD BOOKS

First published in Great Britain in 2023 by Hodder & Stoughton

13 5 7 9 10 8 6 4 2

Text copyright © Working Partners Limited, 2023
Illustrations copyright © Working Partners Limited, 2023
Series created by Working Partners Limited

The moral rights of the author and illustrator have been asserted.

A CIP catalogue record for this book
is available from the British Library.

ISBN 978 1 40836 752 0

Printed and bound in Great Britain by Clays Ltd, Elcograf S.p.A.

The paper and board used in this book are made from wood from responsible sources.

Orchard Books
An imprint of
Hachette Children's Group
Part of Hodder & Stoughton Limited
Carmelite House
50 Victoria Embankment
London EC4Y 0DZ

An Hachette UK Company
www.hachette.co.uk
www.hachettechildrens.co.uk

Daisy Meadows
Author of Rainbow Magic

PiXiE Magic

Dotty and the Sweet Surprise

Illustrated by
Jo Lindley

Meet the Characters

Alice loves all sorts of arts and crafts. She's great at thinking up clever ways to solve problems, and her inventions are amazing!

Alice

Leo

Leo is always kind and thoughtful. When he's not busy helping his friends or practising his juggling, he loves making things in the craft studio with Alice!

Twinkle

Twinkle the firefly is a Glitterbug –
one of the Pixies' minibeast helpers.
The Glitterbugs collect special bits
and bobs for the Pixies to use.

Dotty

Dotty the Pottery Pixie uses
her magical tools to make
gorgeous ceramics that
help fix people's problems.

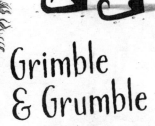

Grimble
& Grumble

The horrible Nixies,
Grimble and Grumble,
live in a rubbish dump
and love casting
bad spells to spoil
everyone's fun.

Leo's house

Playground

Post Office

Alice's flat

Crystal Bay

Dotty's
workshop

The Hive

Cobbletown

Contents

When things are old and start to fray,
Some people just throw them away.
But to us, they aren't quite done:
We see the heart inside each one.

With our friends, the Glitterbugs,
A little magic, and some love,
We turn old things into new.
Will you come and help us too?

Love from
The Pixies

Chapter One
Christmas Sparkle

It was late afternoon in Crystal Bay, and the park looked spectacular. Fairy lights hung in all the trees, sparkling brightly against the darkening sky. The old iron lamps that lined the park's paths flickered on, lighting the way for visitors to the Christmas Eve Fair. The air was frosty, so everyone was well wrapped up. Some people headed for the reindeer roundabout or the ice rink, while others tried games or bought gifts at the stalls.

Two of the most excited people in Crystal Bay at that moment were best friends Alice and Leo, who were running their own craft stall.

"Roll up! Come and make your pompom snowmen!" Leo cried, leaning over the front of the stall and waving at passers-by.

"All the money goes to charity!" Alice called out.

The friends beamed at one another. They loved making all sorts of crafts, so having their own stall was a dream come true.

A small boy in an orange bobble hat approached the stall, smiling shyly.

"Can I make a snowman?"

he asked.

"Of course!" said Leo.

The boy dropped some coins in their bucket, then Alice helped him stick an orange felt nose on his snowman. "How about some red buttons?" she asked, giving him three circles of felt.

"Would your snowman like a woolly top hat?" Leo asked.

"Yes, please!" said the boy. Leo showed him how to fix the hat on with a couple of stitches. Then Alice gave him a tiny scarf and mittens to stick on.

"Wow!" cried the boy, sounding thrilled. "I can put it on our Christmas tree tonight. Thank you!" He bounced off to show his dad.

As well as preparing pompom snowmen, Alice and Leo had spent weeks in their craft shed in Leo's garden, making Christmas presents for their friends and families.

"I can't wait to deliver these gifts after the fair," said Alice. She sniffed the air. "Mmm, what a lovely smell."

"Which one?" Leo laughed. "I can smell roast chestnuts, mince pies, gingerbread and . . ."

"Hot chocolate, kiddos!" said a voice. It was Leo's dad. He walked over to

them, carrying two steaming mugs.

"Thanks!" said Alice and Leo as they wrapped their hands around the cups.

Leo's dad peered into their charity bucket. "You've made lots of money," he said. "But have you had a chance to look around the stalls?"

"A few," said Leo, licking chocolate foam from his lips. "I'd like to try to make candles like those." He pointed to the stall opposite, where candles of all shapes and colours stood in groups.

"See the origami dragon at the front of that stall over there?" said Alice, pointing down the row. "I'd love to be able to make something like that."

"You two and your crafting." Leo's dad chuckled. "Make sure you visit Leo's mum and me over at the photo booth we're running when you get a chance!"

After his dad had left, Leo spotted one of their friends from school. "Look, Alice, it's Oliver!" he said. Leo waved to Oliver, but he didn't notice.

Alice was about to call, "Hi!" when she realised Oliver was with his younger sister, Ivy. They both looked very cross.

"They're having an argument," said Leo.

"I hope they make up soon."

He and Alice didn't want to eavesdrop, so they turned back to their stall. But Oliver and Ivy were arguing so loudly, they couldn't help overhearing.

"You said you'd come ice skating with me," said Ivy. "You promised! But now you say you won't, and you know I'm not

allowed to go by myself!"

Her brother scowled. "We've spent all day doing things you want to do," he said. "It's my turn for some fun. Stop behaving like a brat."

Ivy folded her arms and scowled back. "Huh!" she said, and stormed off to their mum's face-painting stall.

Oliver looked upset, so Alice called him over. "Don't worry about Ivy," she said. "You two can make up when she calms down."

But Oliver shook his head crossly. "I don't want to make up with her," he said, frowning. "It's not *my* fault she isn't allowed to skate by herself."

"But if you don't make up, it will spoil your Christmas," said Leo. "Why not do it now?"

Oliver sighed. "OK, I know it was mean of me not to take Ivy skating but I really wanted to try out the photo booth. Now she's so upset with me I don't think she'll listen even if I do apologise."

Leo watched Oliver trudge away past the candle stall, where a row of lit candles twinkled in glass jars. He noticed that one candle flame was a bright orange, and it wasn't flickering – it was blinking. "That's weird," he said to Alice. "That's not a flame, and it can't be one fairy light on its own."

The blinking light rose from the candle. It circled above Oliver's head, then flew to the face-painting stall and circled around Ivy.

"It's a firefly!"

cried Alice.

"It's a very sparkly firefly," said Leo, twisting around to watch it. "It's orange . . . and

silver . . . and it's leaving a trail of gold sparkles. Alice, it must be a Glitterbug, from Cobbletown!"

Cobbletown was a magical place that Leo and Alice loved to visit. The beautiful Glitterbugs that lived there sparkled like jewels. They came to Crystal Bay to find old treasures that weren't wanted any more, and took them back to Cobbletown. Clever little Pixies used their crafting skills to turn those objects into new, magical things with the power to fix human problems.

Leo clutched Alice's hand. "Glitterbugs look out for people in

Crystal Bay who need help, don't they?"

"Yes!" Alice whispered excitedly. "This Glitterbug must have seen Oliver and Ivy quarrelling. That's why it flew around them."

The Glitterbug landed among the pompoms and looked up at them. Tiny golden stars streamed from its antennae.

"I think it wants us to go back to Cobbletown," said Leo.

"Yes," said Alice, "to get some Pixie help for Ivy and Oliver!"

Their eyes shone with excitement as they

asked the candle sellers to keep an eye on the snowman stall.

"We'll only be gone a minute or so," Leo told them. No time passed in Crystal Bay while they were in Cobbletown!

The sparkly firefly flew through the park gate. Alice and Leo ran after it towards the beach, hurrying beneath Crystal Bay's festive lights. They headed for a wall that was painted with a faded mural of Crystal Bay. Alice and Leo knew that when they looked closely, it wouldn't look *exactly* like Crystal Bay.

As they drew near, the mural's colours brightened and

they saw that snow lay over the roofs of the painted cottages and shops. "It's winter in Cobbletown, too," Alice said excitedly.

The Glitterbug flew straight at the wall and vanished. Alice and Leo knew where it had gone, but they still felt a thrill of excitement to see magic actually happening!

A moment later, the Glitterbug appeared in the painted mural before them, flying around in tiny circles and looping the loop.

Leo and Alice joined hands and jumped right after it.

WHOOOOOOSH!

They zoomed into a rushing wind, faster and faster, until they could see nothing but magical sparkles.

Seconds later, they were standing on firm ground. When the sparkles cleared, they saw . . .

Cobbletown!

Chapter Two
Dotty's Idea

Leo and Alice gazed around in delight.
The pathways were lit by twinkling fairy
lights. There were Christmas trees in
gardens, and above the doors hung
colourful banners that read:

SEASON'S GREETINGS

Alice's eyes sparkled. "It's Christmas in Cobbletown, too," she cried.

Leo spotted a new building that hadn't been there before. It was made from an old biscuit tin, and was twice his height, with a white frosted roof and sparkly jellies stuck all over it. "Wow!" he said. "That's enormous!"

Alice giggled. "It's not enormous –
we've shrunk! Remember, we shrink
when we come to Cobbletown, and go
back to our normal size when we return
to Crystal Bay!"

They watched for the Glitterbug
as they made their way towards the
town centre. There were lots of cute
buildings to look at, all covered in a
layer of cotton-wool snow! Everything in
Cobbletown was carefully handmade
by the Pixies, using objects the
Glitterbugs brought them.

The sweet shop was made from a pink
and yellow doll's house, and it had a

sign over the front door saying:

CANDY COTTAGE

The house's window frames had been mended with lolly sticks, and a cotton reel replaced the missing chimney.

"Look!" said Alice. "The Pixies have strung paper snowflakes between the buildings!"

"And here's a little theatre, all ready for a Christmas show," said Leo.

The Cobbletown Theatre was made from a blue toybox decorated with strands of fairy lights. It was topped by a glistening silver star.

"I spy a new building," said Alice. "I can smell it, too!"

Leo looked where she was pointing. "A gingerbread house!" he said. "Doesn't it look delicious? There'll be enough gingerbread for everyone to share after Christmas!"

The whole town sparkled like frost in sunlight. The friends passed an upturned red fire bucket with a gently smoking chimney. It had a stairway winding up around the outside, making it look a bit like a helter skelter. A Christmas tree, made from pine cones,

stood at the foot of the stairs, and a
glittery sign read:

BUCKET INN.
ALL WELCOME!

Leo glanced around. "Cobbletown's
so quiet. Where is everyone?"

The orange and silver firefly suddenly
appeared, looking just as sparkly, but
much larger than before – he was
almost as big as Leo's hand. He flew
around their heads and headed off into
town.

Alice broke into a run.

"After that Glitterbug!"

The firefly led them to the town square. In the middle was a tall object that was bigger than the other buildings. It looked like a great glittery beehive. Lots of colourful creatures with large eyes and pointed ears were gathered around it. They were the magical Pixies of Cobbletown!

One of the Pixies spotted Leo and Alice and ran over. She had green hair and pink skin, and wore lots of jingling

beaded bracelets on her wrists. It was
Emerald the Jewellery Pixie.

"Come and see!"

she said. "We're decorating the Hive! At
least, the Glitterbugs are!"

The Hive was where the Glitterbugs
brought the objects they collected.
Inside there were lots of little pockets all
around the walls, where everything was
stored. Anyone could help themselves
to whatever they needed to make
something useful or beautiful – or both!

The wintry sun cast a warm glow
through the Hive. It was surrounded

by Glitterbugs – ladybirds, moths, dragonflies, crickets and many more minibeasts. They were taking decorations from the Pixies and putting them on the Hive.

More Pixies ran to greet the two friends.

"Hi, Alice! Hi, Leo!"

"It's great to see you!"

"We're having so much fun!" cried a Pixie with rainbow-striped hair. She showed them some streamers made from sparkly fabric and sequins. "We make all the Christmas decorations for Cobbletown ourselves," she explained.

Emerald the Jewellery Pixie showed them the baubles she'd made by recycling the beads from bracelets and necklaces. Another Pixie wearing paint-splattered clothes had a box of old animal figurines that he'd covered in silver paint and gold sparkles.

One of the Pixies began chanting, and all the others joined in.

"TWINKLE! TWINKLE! MAGIC SPRINKLE!"

The orange and silver firefly flew to the top of the Hive.

"OOOOOO-WEEEEEE!"

he squeaked. The other Glitterbugs joined him. Stars showered from their antennae in golden fountains. They scattered all over the Hive and hung there, like tiny fairy lights. Alice and Leo gasped. The Hive looked just like a beautiful Christmas tree.

"Oooh!" exclaimed everyone.

The firefly Glitterbug zoomed around the Hive, then started rolling in the cotton-wool snow, squeaking happily.

Only the Pixies could understand Glitterbug language. The Pixie with rainbow-coloured hair laughed as she explained, "Twinkle here says the snow we make is much better than the real thing. He hates being cold."

"It's actually quite snuggly," Alice said, bending down to touch the cotton-wool snow with her fingertips.

Emerald asked curiously, "Alice, what

brings you to Cobbletown today?"

"We followed Twinkle because our friend Oliver needs help," Alice explained. "He's fallen out with his sister, Ivy. He wants to make up, but he doesn't think she'll listen to him."

"I see," said Emerald. "So Oliver and Ivy need help to get over their quarrel."

Leo nodded. "They need it today," he said, "otherwise their family's Christmas will be ruined."

Alice looked around at the Pixies and Glitterbugs who had gathered to listen. "Please will you make a magical object to help Oliver say sorry to Ivy?"

There was a chorus of squeaks, tweets and hums from the Glitterbugs, as all the Pixies said, "Yes!"

One voice added, "I have an idea already!"

A Pixie skipped forward. She had peach-coloured skin and a mop of bright pink curly hair. Her spotty ceramic hair accessories couldn't stop those curls from bouncing! The Pixie wore a blue-patterned jumpsuit that reminded Alice of the best china that her mums kept in a glass cabinet for special occasions.

"I'm Dotty the Pottery Pixie," she said with a beaming smile.

"Hi, Dotty!" said Leo. "We'd love to hear your idea."

"I could make pottery mugs for your friends," said the Pixie. "Matching Hug Mugs!"

"That sounds great," Alice said. "Their own

special mugs . . . But how could mugs help Oliver and Ivy to get over their argument?"

Dotty smiled. "Easy! When they share mugs of hot chocolate, the magic will remind them of how much they care about each other. Then they'll hug and make up!"

The Pixies clapped and the Glitterbugs jiggled, fluttered and danced.

"What a brilliant idea!" said Leo.

"Thanks, Dotty," said Alice. "We'll help gather the things you need to make the mugs."

"I have some already," Dotty said,

showing them one of the objects she held. It had a wooden handle like a paintbrush, but both ends were oddly shaped. "This is my modelling tool," she said. "It's for shaping clay. I use the point for making Dotty dots!"

Leo and Alice knew that every Pixie had three magical tools that they always kept with them.

Next, Dotty showed them a tool with a sponge tip. "This is for smoothing clay," she said. Then she brought out her third tool – a small tin. "There's glaze in here, for colouring my pottery."

"We'll need some clay," said Alice.

Dotty beamed. "I have plenty at home," she said. "I collect it from the Clay Caves. But let's grab a few things from the Hive before we start. Come on!"

She skipped inside the Hive, followed by Alice, Leo and Twinkle.

The pockets around the Hive walls bulged with useful items. "We need colourful things to make a lovely glaze," Dotty said. She picked up a large blue-green marble. "Like this."

Leo wondered how Dotty would ever get the marble into her little glaze tin!

Alice found a necklace. "What about

this?" she said. "My mum has a necklace like this one. It shimmers in sunlight."

"Perfect," said Dotty. "So is that," she added, pointing to a silver ribbon that Leo was holding. "I think we have enough—"

Just then, the sound of tiny bells jingle-jangled around the square.

"Someone's coming," Dotty said.

They went outside, where a chilly wind blew around Alice and Leo. They shivered. A mouldy smell filled the air and there were frightened cries from the Pixies:

"It's the Nixies!"

"Dotty, stand behind us," Leo said. "Grimble and Grumble are coming!"

Chapter Three
Nixie Trouble

A windy whirl of rubbish arrived first –
paper scraps, dead leaves and so on.

Then the Nixies appeared. Grimble

was tall and skinny, while Grumble was

short and wide. They were both bigger

than Alice and Leo, and towered over

the Pixies. The Nixies were scowling, as

usual, but there was something different
about them this time . . .

Both Nixies wore long, dirty fake
beards, and each had a mud-splattered
red hat over their greasy hair. The
Santa outfits they wore were covered in
food stains and they held frayed ropes

attached to a tatty old sleigh. Rusty

bells dangled from their lumpy ears.

Grumble laughed. "Ho ho! We brought

you all a sleigh full of presents!"

He and Grimble tilted the sleigh and

tipped everything out.

CRASH!

China smashed.

EEEEE!

Metal scraped.

SPLAT!

Dirty pans spilled out mouldy food.

Scraps of plastic, tin and wood scattered over the square. Shreds of torn paper drifted about. A sheet of smelly fish-and-chip wrapping blew against Leo's leg. He screwed it up and plonked it back in the sleigh. "These things are junk, not gifts!" he cried.

"They're messing up our town," Dotty whimpered.

Alice hated to see the little Pixie upset. She turned to Grumble and Grimble. "You might live on a rubbish tip," she shouted, "but there's no need to dump your filth in Cobbletown. You're ruining Christmas!"

"But we love Christmas," giggled Grumble. "So many gifts to break!"

"So much fun to spoil!" Grimble sneered.

"We won't let you wreck things," Leo said. "Go home!"

The Nixies reached for the magic hammers in their belts.

"Get back, everyone!" Alice cried.

Before anyone could move, Grimble and Grumble pointed their hammers at Twinkle.

"OOO-WEEEEE!"

he squeaked, and

flapped his
wings. But he
was too slow.

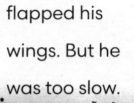

ZZZAPPP!

Dark, evil-
smelling sparks
shot towards Twinkle
and crackled around him.

Dotty buried her face in her hands
as the Glitterbug's sparkly orange and
silver faded. His light dimmed and
flickered as he turned a dull grey.

Alice groaned. "Grimble and Grumble

have turned Twinkle into a Gloomybug."

But the Nixies hadn't finished. They leaned over the Gloomybug until their knobbly noses almost touched his antennae. "See the Dotty Pixie's magic tools?" Grimble said.

Dotty clutched her tools tightly.

The Pixies wailed and Emerald cried out, "Don't steal them, you meanies!"

Grumble grinned. "Nixies wouldn't *dream* of stealing tools," he said.

"Course we wouldn't," said Grimble. Her filthy face swooped down to Twinkle again. "*You* steal her tools!"

Alice and Leo tried to shield Dotty

from the
Gloomybug,
but he zoomed
around them
and snatched the
tools from Dotty's
arms.

"No!" she cried.

"Good
Gloomybug,"
Grimble said in a
voice that sounded
like syrup with sand in
it. "Go to Crystal Bay.
Hide the tools where

they'll never be found."

"Twinkle, don't!" cried Alice, Leo and the Pixies. The Glitterbugs squeaked and twittered and their antennae drooped as the Gloomybug flew away.

"Heh! Heh!" laughed the Nixies. The wind began to blow. It swirled and whirled, whipping straw and cobwebs and sticky fluff from the purple hair that stuck out from under their silly hats. The whirlwind grew stronger and dirtier and, in seconds, Grumble and Grimble had disappeared from view.

Everyone paused to take a deep breath. Then the Pixies ran to Dotty, and the Glitterbugs scurried, crawled and fluttered back to the Hive.

Alice and Leo held Dotty's shaking hands. Her eyes glistened with tears. "I can't make magical pottery without my tools," she said in a wobbly voice. "I won't be able to help Oliver or anyone else, ever again!"

"You will!" said Leo. "Alice and I will see to that. Does Twinkle look after Crystal Bay Park?"

Dotty nodded. "Yes, it's his favourite place. He loves watching the old iron lampposts light up in the evenings."

"Then that's where we'll go," said

Alice. "There's no time to lose."

Dotty patted her tears away. "Me, too?" she asked.

"You, too," said Leo.

The other Pixies waved goodbye as they raced back to where they'd arrived in Cobbletown. On the wall was a mural of Crystal Bay. As they drew near, it came to life. Christmas lights twinkled in the painted park, and the reindeer roundabout turned.

"Hurry," said Alice. "A tiny grey Gloomybug will be hard to see in the busy fair. We need to get on his tail quickly."

The friends held hands, ran to the mural and jumped towards the park gate. As they tumbled into a whirl of magical sparkles, Alice felt the wind tousle her hair.

When the sparkles began to clear, they felt firm ground beneath their feet.

Alice and Leo were back to their normal size. Dotty, who was only as tall as a toothbrush, was in danger of being trodden on, so Alice carefully lifted her into Leo's hood.

"Ooh, cosy," Dotty said. "Oh! Is that your Christmas Fair? It looks exciting!"

"Watch for Twinkle, Dotty," said Leo. "We'll circle the fair first, and check the lampposts that he loves."

They followed the park railings, which were decorated with strands of fairy lights.

Alice stopped suddenly and pointed to where a dim fairy light seemed to be flickering. "Could that be—?"

"Twinkle!" Dotty stood up, holding on to one of Leo's ears. "It's Twinkle!" she cried.

The Gloomybug took off, with grey dust streaming behind him instead of his normal sparkly gold trail.

"He's holding my magical sponge!" cried Dotty.

Alice ran ahead. "Twinkle's heading for the ice rink," she called back.

Leo followed to where skaters whizzed around the ice, laughing and chatting.

"I can't see

him," said Alice, scanning the rink.

A group of small children went by, holding on tight to Polar Bear Pals. The sliding frames with jolly white bears on the front helped them to skate safely.

"There!" Leo pointed to a skater in blue joggers and a red bobble hat. Twinkle was flying above her. He dropped down and perched on the hat, showering it with grey dust. The skater skated on. She didn't know she had a passenger!

"If we're going to catch that Gloomybug," Alice said, "we'd better get our skates on."

Chapter Four
Polar Bear Pals

Leo and Alice stepped on to the ice.

"Are you OK in my hood, Dotty?" Leo asked.

"I'm snuggly warm," the Pixie replied. "Go faster!"

Alice laughed. "Careful – not *too* fast!" she said. "We might miss the skater with the red bobble hat."

Dotty suddenly grabbed tufts of Leo's hair and turned his head to the left.

"There she is!" Leo cried.

"No," said Alice, pointing the other way. "She's over there."

"But . . ." Leo began. "Oh no! Several skaters have red bobble hats. How can we tell which one Twinkle's on?"

They circled the rink, taking care not to bump into little children with Polar Bear Pals. Then Leo gave a shout. "There! Twinkle's just flown to a different hat – a blue one."

They watched the Gloomybug burrow

into the hat's fluffy bobble.

"He's looking for somewhere to hide Dotty's sponge tool," Alice said. "I hope he doesn't spot us. He might fly away over the trees." Then she glanced back at the small children wobbling along. "I've an idea," she said.

Alice took Leo to the edge of the rink and borrowed two Polar Bear Pals. "We can stoop down behind these," she said, "then Twinkle won't see us following him."

"Brilliant!" said Leo.

They set off, keeping as low as possible, and

soon spotted Twinkle perched
on the blue hat. He still had
Dotty's magical sponge and
he was looking around.
Suddenly he zipped
across to another
hat. It was beige
and the bobble
was nearly as big
as the hat.

Alice and Leo
could see that
Twinkle was
shivering.
Snowflakes

spilled out from his antennae.

"He won't like being so cold," said Dotty.

The Gloomybug snuggled into the fluffy bobble, which was almost the same colour as the sponge.

"Gosh, if we hadn't seen him fly there, we'd never have noticed the sponge," said Leo. "It's well camouflaged."

"That's probably why he chose it," said Alice.

The beige-hatted skater had a Polar Bear Pal, too, and she was going quite fast. Her matching scarf streamed out behind her.

Leo chased after her. He was about to grab the sponge when he noticed Oliver skating nearby. So instead, he whispered to Dotty, "I don't want Oliver to see what I'm up to. Can you catch the end of the scarf? Maybe you can climb up it and take the sponge."

The Pixie tried, but she pulled the scarf a little too hard and the skater looked around.

It was Ivy!

Leo froze. Had she seen Dotty?

But Ivy was staring at Oliver. "That was you!" she said. "You pulled my scarf!"

"I didn't!" exclaimed Oliver. "I'm

nowhere near you!"

"Did!"

"Didn't!"

Alice whispered to Leo. "This is making their argument even worse," she said. "Oh, look, Twinkle's on the move!"

The Gloomybug had appeared from his nest in the beige bobble. He flew off, leaving the sponge behind.

"Quick, Dotty!" said Leo. "He thinks the sponge is safely hidden. Try again while Ivy's squabbling with Oliver."

He skated close behind Ivy, still crouching down. Dotty leaned out of

Leo's hood, took hold of Ivy's scarf and scrambled up it. Ivy didn't notice a thing!

The Pixie burrowed into the fluffy bobble and pulled out her magical sponge.

Just then, Ivy tossed her head, saying, "Go away, Oliver!"

Dotty tumbled off the hat and fell into Leo's waiting hands. Alice lifted her back into Leo's hood and they skated off.

"Whew!" said Alice, as they returned the Polar Bear Pals. "We've got the first magical tool."

Dotty beamed with delight. "Only two more to get," she said. "Let's go!"

"But we don't know where Twinkle's gone," said Leo. "The fair's so crowded. How can we spot him?" People were gathered in groups around stalls, or queuing for rides, or just wandering about eating toffee apples and candy floss. "We've no idea where he'll hide the other tools," Leo added.

Dotty's face fell.

Alice hugged her. "We won't give up," she said. "We *will* find those tools." She glanced at Leo and whispered, "But I'm not sure how."

Chapter Five
Fairy Lights to the Rescue

Leo, Alice and Dotty were still searching

for Twinkle when they met Oliver again,

beneath a sign saying:

Oliver looked upset. "I thought ice

skating with Ivy would sort everything

out," he said. "She really wanted me to skate with her. But now she's left the rink, and I can't find her."

"Perhaps she's in the grotto," said Alice. "Let's look."

Leo pulled her back. "What about . . ." he began. But Alice whispered, "Twinkle may be in there. It's worth trying."

They followed a path between rocky walls. As it widened out, they gasped. All around the edges of a clearing were ice sculptures, sparkling as they reflected the fairy lights that hung all around. There was a swan, an angel with outstretched wings and a Christmas pudding topped with ice holly. Leo and Alice would have loved to look at them all, but they had to find Twinkle.

A tall Christmas tree stood in the clearing. It was decorated with brightly coloured baubles, painted pine cones, candy canes and artificial snow. On top was a glittering golden star.

"It's lovely," Dotty whispered.

"Beautiful," said Alice. "I bet Ivy would love to see it."

A small face beneath a beige bobble hat peered around from the other side of the tree.

"I *can* see it, Alice," Ivy said with a cheeky grin.

She scowled when she noticed Oliver, and ran off, calling over her shoulder, "I'm not talking to you."

Oliver sighed. "I wish I could make things right," he said, walking out of the grotto with his head down.

Leo tugged Alice's sleeve and showed

her an ice sculpture of a reindeer. Grey dust was scattered between its antlers. "Twinkle's been here," he said excitedly.

"Ooh," said Dotty. "Maybe he's hidden my tools here."

Several more sculptures were sprinkled with grey dust, but there was no sign of the tools. Leo examined a sculpture of Father Christmas with an icy sack at his feet. The top was open so people could see the ice presents inside.

There was grey dust in the ice-sculpture sack. And wedged between two icy gifts was Dotty's modelling tool!

"Hooray!" cried Dotty. "Pull it out."

Leo tried, but his hand couldn't fit inside the sack, so Alice had a go. She grasped the tip of the tool, but it was jammed in tightly. "I can't get a proper grip," she said, rubbing her cold hands.

"Lift me down," said Dotty. "My little hands should do it."

The friends held her so she could reach into the sack. She took hold of the tool and pulled. "It won't budge," she said. "It's frozen into the ice. Now what?"

Alice thought for a moment. "Wait

here," she said, and sped away. A minute later she was back, carrying a string of fairy lights with a little battery pack attached.

"These were wound around a bush," she said. "No one will mind us borrowing them."

She switched on the fairy lights and held them close to the Pixie's modelling tool.

"I don't understand . . ." Dotty began. Then she said, "*Oh!* Yes, I do! The warmth from the lights is melting the edges of the presents, next to my magical modelling tool."

Leo grinned. "You can trust Alice's inventing skills to solve a problem," he said. "Dotty, get ready to pull."

A moment later, the tool popped free. Dotty waved it in the air. "Hooray!"

"Two down, one to go," said Leo.

They'd just returned the lights when Alice noticed a movement in a nearby tree. It was Twinkle! He was shivering so much that he was struggling to hold the glaze tin.

"Look," she whispered, pointing.

"Twinkle!" Dotty cried.

"Sshh!" said Alice. But it was too late.

He'd seen them.

"OOWEEE!

OO-WEEE!"

Twinkle squeaked.

"OO-OO-OO-WEEE!"

"He sounds angry," said Leo. "And by the look of him, he must be freezing."

The Gloomybug flexed his wings.

"Oh no," said Alice. "He's going to fly off. We must follow him until we have a chance to rescue the tin – or talk him into giving it back."

Dotty shook her head.

"Now that Twinkle is

under a Nixie spell, he'll just stay mean and bad," she said. "Gloomybugs can't help it."

Leo felt sorry for Twinkle. "It must be horrible being so cold," he said. "I wish we could catch him and take him somewhere warm."

Twinkle managed to get a grip on the tin. He flapped his wings, then took off.

"Quick!" cried Dotty. "If he drops my tin, someone might pick it up, or it could fall into—"

Alice didn't hear any more, because Leo was racing through the crowds with Dotty in his hood. She chased after them. It was growing darker, which made the lampposts and fairy lights so much brighter. *It will be hard to spot a Gloomybug's dim tail light*, she thought, as she caught up with the others.

Leo looked desperate. "We've lost him," he said.

"Don't worry, I'm sure we can find him again," said Alice, trying to sound more confident than she felt.

Then Leo noticed a dim light at

the top of the tall Christmas tree.

"Something's flying around the star," he

said. "It must be Twinkle!"

Chapter Six
All the Way to the Star!

"Hurry! Let's catch him," said Leo, starting forward.

"Careful," said Alice. "If Twinkle sees us, he'll fly away."

"But if we don't catch him, we'll never get my tin back," said Dotty, with a tremor in her voice. "And poor Twinkle might stay a Gloomybug forever."

Leo patted the Pixie's tiny hand. "Then all we can do is try to break the Nixies' horrible spell," he said. "We've done it before. We must do something kind for Twinkle, but we have to take care – only the right act of kindness will break the spell."

Alice looked thoughtful. "He's really suffering from the cold," she said. "The kindest thing would be to help him get warm."

"That's a great idea!" said Leo. "And guess who has lots of tiny woollen clothes, just the right size for Twinkle?"

Alice thought for a moment and then bobbed up and down. "We do! At our stall!"

"Exactly." Leo grinned. "Dotty, you keep watch and we'll be back in a moment!"

Dotty hid behind the reindeer ice sculpture, and Leo wrapped his scarf around her to keep her warm.

Then he and Alice hurried to their stall
and stuffed their pockets with all sorts
of woolly objects, before racing back to
Dotty.

"Look at all those people!" Dotty said,
pointing.

The Crystal Bay Singers were standing
in front of the tree, leafing through their
music booklets. Visitors were gathering,
waiting to hear their favourite Christmas
songs.

"Did you see where Twinkle landed?"
Alice asked.

"Yes," said Dotty. "I'm afraid he's right
at the top of the tree."

Leo looked at the star. "We'd need a long ladder to get up there," he said. "Anyway, we can't do that. The singers would see us, and they'd think we were doing something naughty."

Alice frowned. "We have to do it – somehow."

Dotty took a tiny terracotta charm from her apron pocket. It was star-shaped and speckled with golden dots. "This is my emergency magic," she said. "Both of you, touch it."

When they did as she said, a shivery feeling ran right through Alice and Leo and a burst of sparkles surrounded them. When the sparkles disappeared, they found they were the same size as Dotty.

"You shrank us!" said Leo.

"I did, didn't I?" Dotty said proudly.

"But why?" asked Alice, as the singers began "Little Donkey".

"Because now we can climb up the tree after Twinkle," said Dotty. "If we go around the back, the crowd won't see us."

"Clever Dotty!" said Leo.

They crept to the back of the tree and clambered on to the lowest branches.

The sharp scent of pine filled their nostrils. "Mmm, what a Christmassy smell," said Alice, as she wriggled around a wooden soldier. The baubles quivered, but none of them fell off. A strand of tinsel tickled Dotty's nose and made her sneeze,

but the singers were so loud that no one heard.

Leo was deep in the tree, near the trunk. All he could see were pine branches, Christmas ornaments and tinsel. It was like being in his own private winter wonderland!

They climbed past reindeer ornaments, bells, Christmas elves and chocolate penguins. When Alice paused to catch her breath, she glanced down. The ground was a long way away! She wasn't sure she wanted to climb any higher, but then she thought of poor Twinkle under that horrible spell. She started off again and caught up with the others. They had reached a gap where the next branch was too high to climb on to.

Dotty jumped and her fingers just touched the branch, but she couldn't get a grip. Down she tumbled, crying, "Help!"

Alice and Leo each grabbed an arm as Dotty fell.

"Whew!" she said. "That wasn't a good idea."

Alice looked thoughtful. "Let me try something," she said. She reached for a

striped

candy cane,

stretched up and

hooked it over the

higher branch. Then

she pulled it down

towards Leo and

Dotty.

"Climb on it," she

said. "Quickly!"

Dotty and Leo

clambered on to

the branch, then Alice pulled herself up the candy cane. Just when she thought she was going to slide back down, four hands grabbed her and hauled her up.

"Thanks!" she said.

On they climbed, until there were only a few branches to go.

The Crystal Bay Singers had just finished "We Wish You a Merry Christmas", and were having a break. Alice froze when one of the choir looked straight at her.

"Stay still!" she whispered without moving her lips.

Leo and Dotty held their breath.

The singer spoke to the woman next to him, saying, "I do believe one of those elf ornaments moved."

Several people looked up.

The man laughed. "Silly me!" he said. "The wind probably blew it. They're just cute little decorations."

"Very realistic ones," said the woman.

"Ahem!" said their leader, and the singers launched into "Jingle Bells".

"Whew!" said Leo. "That was close."

They climbed on. As they drew near the star, they heard a faint

"OO-OO-OO-OO-OO."

Alice rested against the tree's trunk. "Twinkle sounds as if he's shivering," she said. "What's he saying, Dotty?"

The Pixie listened. "Oh dear," she said. "He says he's never been so miserable. His wings are so stiff that he can't flap them. He wishes he was warm and says it's no fun being a Gloomybug."

Little snowflakes drifted over the friends.

"He'll be even colder now it's snowing," Leo said. "Poor Twinkle."

Dotty peeped up through the branches. "It's not snowing," she said. "Those snowflakes are coming from his antennae. He's very unhappy."

"Come on then," said Alice. "It's time to warm that frosty firefly up!"

Chapter Seven
Magical Mugs

The Gloomybug shivered so much that
his branch shook.

"OOOOO-OO-WE-EE,"

he squeaked.

Alice took some little hats and scarves
from her pocket, and Leo brought out

tiny socks and mittens.

"Twinkle?" Alice said gently. "Come and get warm."

The Gloomybug's antennae twitched. He saw what Alice and Leo held and tried to flex his wings, but he was too cold to fly. He had to crawl towards them.

"He's coming," Leo whispered. "Let's hold them nearer, so he can reach." Aloud he said, "Help yourself, Twinkle. These will warm you up."

"We know you hate being cold," said Dotty. "We want to make you cosy."

The Gloomybug snatched some

mittens, a scarf and a little orange hat. He tried to put mittens on his legs, but he was too cold and stiff. Alice stretched out and helped ease his legs into two green mittens and four red ones. She wound a soft scarf around his grey body and put the woolly hat on his head. He was completely bundled up.

Leo grinned. "He's like a shivery ball of wool," he said. "All I can see are his antennae."

Twinkle soon grew

still. He sighed and squeaked,

"OO-WEEE-OOOOO!"

"Hooray!" said Dotty. "He says he's snuggly warm."

"Look," said Alice, pointing to the back of the fluffy bundle that was Twinkle. A faint glow shone through the wool.

"His tail light's growing brighter!" said Leo.

A shower of tiny golden stars spilled from Twinkle's antennae.

Alice gasped. "The spell's broken!"

"Hooray!" Dotty and Leo cried.

"Ssh!" Leo giggled. "People will

wonder why the Christmas tree is cheering!"

Two green mittens appeared from inside the scarf. They held Dotty's glaze tin.

"OO-WEE,"

Twinkle said. His head appeared, then his body. It was shimmering orange and silver again. Alice and Leo high-fived.

"Whoopee!" said Dotty. "Twinkle, you're not a Gloomybug any more. You're a Glitterbug!"

"Oo-wee oo-wee-wee-wee oo-wee-oo," the firefly squeaked.

Dotty smiled. "He says he's sorry he took my magical tools."

"It wasn't your fault, Twinkle," said Alice. "Grimble and Grumble made you do it."

"OOO-WE-OOO!"

"He says thanks for warming him up," said the Pixie. "He was cold and frightened."

"Time for a group hug!" cried Leo, putting his arm around Alice's shoulders. They'd hugged Pixies before, but they could hardly believe they were also hugging a firefly!

Twinkle pulled the scarf right off. "Oo-oo-wee," he squeaked. "Oo-we-we-we-ooo?"

Dotty explained. "He says he's much warmer now, but can he keep the hat, please? It matches the orange of his body."

Leo laughed. "Of course!" he said.

Twinkle flexed his wings and did a happy loop-the-loop. The hat fell off, but Alice caught it and popped it back on his head. Golden stars showered over her hand.

Dotty clapped in

delight. "Let's go back to Cobbletown and make those magical mugs!"

Alice and Leo gazed at Dotty's home.

It was a huge green vase that looked like it had once been smashed and pieced back together. It was covered in a web of shimmering golden lines.

"It's beautiful!" said Leo.

"My mums tried mending a vase like that once," said Alice. "Mum held the pieces in place while Mo glued them. It looked awful. Nothing like this!"

"Kintsugi is a very special type of craft," Dotty told them. "It's when you repair pottery with gold. It makes the breaks and cracks look beautiful. Those golden lines show a part of the vase's life story."

"And now it has a new life as your home," said Leo. "I'd love to try kintsugi one day!"

As they entered Dotty's perfectly round home, Alice gasped. The walls were decorated with beautiful

mosaics that glittered in the lamplight with rich, glowing colours. "How gorgeous!" she said.

Dotty sat at her potter's wheel. Alice had seen one before, and she glanced beneath Dotty's. "Don't you have something for your foot to start and stop your wheel?" she asked.

Dotty looked puzzled. "No," she said. "I just tell it what to do." She cut a lump of greyish clay with her modelling tool and threw it on the wheel. Then she dampened her hands and said, "Let's go, wheel!"

Sparkles surrounded her, whirling as

fast as the wheel.
They heard
Dotty's voice say,
"OK, wheel, take
a rest."

When the
sparkles
cleared, there
were two mugs,
complete with
handles.

Dotty swept her magical sponge over
the mugs. At once, they changed from
grey into browny-orange.

"Wow!" said Leo. "They're the same

terracotta colour as your magic charm, Dotty."

Alice was astonished. "That's so cool," she said. "When we use clay at school, it has to be fired in a kiln before it hardens and turns that colour."

Dotty frowned. "Ooh, that sounds terribly slow. I'm glad I can use magic!" She tilted her head. "What pattern shall I make?" she wondered. "Swirly, I think. Ooh, I know!" She opened her tin of glaze, then took from her apron pocket the large blue-green marble she'd found at the Hive. She held it over the glaze tin and squeezed, as if she was trying to get juice from a lemon. When Dotty opened her hand, the marble was gone. She did the same with the shimmery necklace that Alice had picked up.

Next, Dotty dipped a paintbrush into the tin and flicked it four or five times at the mugs.

SWISH!

Colour flared in a rainbow explosion, and there were the two mugs, covered in shimmering blue-green swirls.

Alice caught her breath.

"Oliver and Ivy will love

them," she said.

"Shall I add their names?" Dotty asked.

"Yes, please!" said Leo.

Dotty squeezed the silver ribbon Leo had found over the glaze. She dipped her brush into the shining tin and wondered, "Straight lines? Or wiggly? No! Dots, of course!"

She formed the letters with little taps of her brush, murmuring, "O-l-i-v-e-r," then "I-v-y."

When she'd finished, Alice said, "Dotty, you're the most magical potter ever. Let's show Twinkle and the other Pixies."

Outside, everyone gathered to admire Dotty's Hug Mugs. They all agreed that Ivy and Oliver would love them.

Emerald the Jewellery Pixie came to Alice and Leo with her hands behind her back. "We have presents for you," she said, smiling. "Close your eyes and hold out your hands."

The friends were thrilled when they opened their eyes. They each held a beautiful snow globe with a Cobbletown scene inside. There was a cottage, a shop and the nursery school, with

tiny Pixies in fluffy coats building a snowman.

"Thank you, they're lovely!" cried Alice.

"Fantastic! Thanks!" said Leo. "They're beautifully made."

Emerald and the other Pixies giggled. "We all helped," Emerald said.

Leo and Alice shared a worried glance. They hadn't expected presents.

"We're sorry," said Alice. "We don't have anything for you."

The Pixies rushed to hug them, and Dotty said, "You help us keep our magic safe from Grimble and Grumble. That's the best present ever!"

Just then . . .

Jingle! Jangle! Jangle!

"Look out!" cried Leo. "Nixies!"

Chapter Eight
Presents!

The Pixies huddled together, trembling, while the Glitterbugs scurried around in a panic.

Alice and Leo covered their noses and shut their eyes as a smelly, dusty wind whooshed around them. When the wind stopped, they looked up and saw

that Grimble and Grumble were still in
their Father Christmas outfits, but they
looked even grubbier than before.

The Nixies glared at Twinkle.

"Spoiled our plan, you did!" said
Grimble. She stamped so hard that Leo
felt the ground tremble.

Grumble's hairy face swooped down to look Twinkle in the eyes. "You lost that Pixie's tools," he said.

Alice and Leo hurried to protect the Glitterbug. "Leave him alone!" said Alice.

"Ah, this is all your fault!" Grumble growled.

"That's right," said Dotty. "Alice and Leo are good and kind, and helped us."

The Nixies scowled, but Dotty stood her ground. "You did a bad thing, stealing my tools, but it's Christmas, and we think even nasty Nixies deserve a bit of festive magic."

She turned to a Pixie with pearly skin, who held two wrapped gifts. She wore a shell-pink shower cap over long hair that floated in the breeze like feathery seaweed. Her white dress bubbled over her like sea foam. "Come on, Bubbles," said Dotty.

The Pixie offered the gifts to Grimble and Grumble. "I'm Bubbles the Soap Pixie," she said. "I made these especially for you."

The Nixies grunted and took the presents. Bubbles snatched her hands away so their filth didn't touch her shimmering skin.

Grimble and Grumble ripped the paper off. Inside each parcel was a bar of greeny-grey soap.

Leo looked anxiously at Alice. "I don't think the Nixies will like soap," he said quietly. "They love dirt and mess and rotting things. I hope Bubbles won't be upset."

Grimble and Grumble sniffed the soap. They grinned toothy grins.

"Lovely pong!" said Grimble.

As the soap's scent wafted over them, Alice and Leo realised what the Nixies meant. It was as if rotten egg mixed with old Brussels sprouts and smelly socks had been stuffed inside cheesy trainers for a week.

Bubbles whispered, "They only wash once a year, when their Great Aunt Grouchy visits."

"Yuck!" said Alice.

Still sniffing their stinky soap, the Nixies disappeared once more inside the whirling wind.

"OOO-WEEE!"

Twinkle squeaked.

Bubbles giggled. "You're right, Twinkle. They didn't say thank you.'"

The Nixies had left heaps of rubbish behind. The Pixies scurried around, clearing up paper scraps, slimy banana skins and half-chewed hairy toffees.

"We'd love to help," Alice told Dotty, "but we need to get the mugs to Oliver and Ivy."

The little Pixie hugged them both. "Goodbye," she said. "And thank you."

"Bye, Dotty," said Alice and Leo. "Bye, everyone."

Alice tickled Twinkle's antennae. A shower of stars burst out of them, almost hiding him from view.

"OO-WEEEEE!"

he squeaked.

Dotty giggled. "Twinkle says you're the best tree climbers and knitters ever!"

The Pixies gathered to wave Leo and Alice on their way. "Come again soon!" they called.

Once the two friends were back at the mural where they'd arrived in Cobbletown, they put the snow globes in their pockets and tucked the Hug Mugs safely inside their coats. They clasped hands as they tumbled into the mural, then . . .

WHOOOOOOSH!

They were whisked back to Crystal
Bay and the Christmas Fair.

"Right," said Leo, when he'd got his
breath back. "Time to fix Oliver and Ivy's
quarrel."

"Let's split up and look for them," said

Alice. "We'll tell them to come to the hot chocolate stand in ten minutes. Keep the mugs hidden!"

They soon found their friends and gave them the message. Oliver looked puzzled, but said, "OK."

Ivy just nodded, as her mouth was full of toffee apple.

At the hot chocolate stand, Leo said, "Two hot chocolates, please, with marshmallows and whipped cream. And please can we have them in these mugs? They're for our friends."

"Oh my," said the lady, "these are very special mugs, aren't they?"

Soon Alice spotted Ivy coming towards them. Then Oliver appeared, threading his way through the crowd.

Alice said to the hot chocolate lady, "The mugs are for those children."

Ivy and Oliver's faces lit up when they were given the hot chocolate. They each thanked the lady, but they didn't speak to one another. They stood with their backs to each other, sipping their drinks.

"I wish they'd turn around," whispered Leo.

But Ivy suddenly said in surprise, "Oh! My name's on this lovely mug."

Oliver turned and looked. "It's nice," he said. "Lucky you."

Ivy pointed to his mug. "That's funny," she said. "Your name's on that one!"

They grinned at each other, then Oliver said. "Sorry I left you at the ice rink."

"I'm sorry I made you do what I wanted all the time, instead of taking turns to choose," said Ivy.

"And I'm sorry for the things I said when we argued," Oliver added.

"Me too," said Ivy.

Leo watched Oliver put his arm around his sister. They hugged, then

started to laugh. Leo turned to Alice.
"What a relief! The argument's over," he
said.

They bumped fists. "We did it!" Alice
said. "Thanks to Pixie Magic!"

Much later, Leo and Alice pulled their almost empty sledge back to Leo's garden and the craft shed. They'd delivered all the homemade gifts to their friends and family. Two parcels remained, which Leo carried into the shed.

They put the snow globes on the windowsill where the morning sun would make them sparkle. Then Alice picked up one of the parcels. The present was decorated with ribbon and a sprig of real holly leaves and berries. "This is for you, Leo," she said. "Happy Christmas!"

"Thanks," said Leo, and he gave her the other present. It was wrapped in white paper, and tied with red, green and silver ribbons that he'd woven together. "Happy Christmas!" he said.

Alice opened her parcel first. Inside was an origami Christmas tree, made by Leo. There was also a pack of colourful origami paper tied up with raffia, and some pictures

of things that Alice could make with the paper. She was thrilled. "Thanks, Leo!" she said. "You knew it was my favourite before I even told you! You're the best friend ever!"

Leo opened his present carefully. Inside was a chunky candle that Alice had made, striped with different colours. "It's gorgeous!" he said. When he found she had also given him wax and wicks and scented oils, he said, "You knew, too! Now I can make my own candles. Thanks, Alice." He grinned. "I'm not the best friend ever – you are!"

They both laughed. "What a great Christmas this is," said Alice. She peered through the window. Snow was falling, white against the night sky. "It looks magical," she said quietly, then shared a grin with Leo.

He opened the window wide. They stuck their heads out and yelled at the tops of their voices . . .

Read on for a sneak preview of
Pippin and the Birthday Bake ...

Chapter One
Cake Attack!

A blustery wind rustled the leaves and rattled the windows of the wooden shed at the bottom of Leo's garden. But inside, all was peaceful.

Leo and Alice sat at their crafting desk, surrounded by boxes and shelves full of paintings, models and sculptures.

They were both so busy that even Leo hadn't said a word in minutes.

Alice frowned with concentration as she threaded the last red-and-blue spotted pennant on to her bunting. She had cut each flag herself from an old dress that used to belong to one of her mums.

"Finished!" she said at last, sitting back. "How are you doing?"

"I'm on the last 'H' . . ." said Leo, without looking up. He was writing big gold letters on a purple banner, using a special glittery pen.

Alice waited, gazing round happily

at the crafting paradise that they had created in the ramshackle old shed. *Our favourite place in the world*, she thought. *No, wait. Second favourite!* Nothing could beat Cobbletown, a secret world that only Alice and Leo knew about, where magical Pixies turned unwanted belongings into magical objects that solved people's problems.

"There!" said Leo. "What do you think?"

A grin spread across Alice's face as she read the finished banner: *Happy Birthday, Hannah!*

"She's going to love it!"

It was their friend Hannah's eighth birthday today, and she had asked them to make the decorations for her party. Alice and Leo couldn't wait to show her what they'd created! Besides the multi-coloured bunting and the banner, they had cut some streamers, decorated napkins and made paper chains out of old magazines.

They had just begun to pack the decorations into a box ready to take to the party along with Hannah's present, when there was a knock at the door.

"Come in!" said Leo.

The door opened, and Alice's mum

Ingrid popped her head inside. "Ready to go, team?"

"Phew!" Alice picked up the decorations. "Just in time."

Leo jiggled and danced across the lawn as Alice followed her mum, carefully carrying the box to the side gate. "Bye, Mum!" Leo called through the kitchen window. "Bye, Dad!" He darted to get the gate for Alice. "This party's going to be amazing!"

Find out what happens next in
Pippin and the Birthday Bake!

Make Your Own Air-Drying Clay!

Dotty uses her magical powers when she works with clay. But even without magic, you can make your own modelling clay with just a few ingredients . . .

Please ask an adult for help with this activity.

You will need:

- 1 cup bicarbonate of soda
- ½ cup cornflour
- ¾ cup water
- Measuring cups
- Saucepan
- Wooden spoon
- Mixing bowl or baking sheet

Optional:

- Rolling pin
- Biscuit cutters
- Paints and paintbrush

Method:

1. Add the ingredients to the saucepan and stir together with the wooden spoon.

2. Ask an adult to cook the mixture over a medium heat, stirring frequently, until it starts to come away from the sides of the pan and takes on the consistency of mashed potato.

3. Remove from the heat and transfer the mixture to a bowl or baking sheet to cool down to room temperature. This will take at least half an hour.

4. The clay should be very soft but not sticky, so dust your work surface with a little more cornflour if required. You can model the clay with your hands or roll it out and cut out shapes using biscuit cutters.

5. When your models are finished, leave them to dry for 3–5 days at room temperature. Once they're fully dry you can paint them, if you like!

6. Leftover clay can be wrapped in plastic film and stored in an airtight container for another time.

Have you read
Emerald and the Friendship Bracelet?